My Giraffe Makes Me Laugh

Marc Schmatjen
Illustrated by: M. Scott Arena

AuthorHouse™
1663 Liberty Drive
Bloomington, IN 47403
www.authorhouse.com
Phone: 1-800-839-8640

First published by AuthorHouse 4/13/2010

ISBN: 978-1-4520-0941-4 (sc)

Library of Congress Control Number: 2010904758

Printed in the United States of America
Bloomington, Indiana

authorHOUSE®

For Jack, Bella, AJ, Joe, and Abby

My Hippopotamus makes a-lot-of-fuss

when we play in the mud and muck.

And it requires quite a-lot-of-us

to get her feet un-stuck.

My Wildebeest likes to feast

on junk food that is yummy.

But he really should eat sprouts and yeast.

They're better for his tummy.

My Porcupine's a friend-of-mine

and he's somewhat tickly.

Most of the time he's oh-so-fine

but he can get quite prickly.

My **Jackal** likes to tackle me

when I come through the door.

He lets out a big ol' cackle

as he takes me to the floor.

My **Antelope** can swing on-a-rope.

She really is a riot.

She does a flip she calls the lope-de-dope

and says, "You ought to try it."

My **Elephant** tripped and fell-and-bent

the front wheel of my bike.

And now because of-the-dent

I'm always turning right.

My **Crocodile** can walk-a-mile

in the sun or in the rain.

But he'd prefer to swim or sleep awhile

if it's all the same.

My **Lion** keeps on tryin'

to sneak out of my room.

I have to keep an eye-on him

or he'll wind up at the zoo.

My Monkey and I get funky

when we dance around the place.

He's so happy and so spunky

he puts a big smile on my face.

My **Giraffe** makes me laugh

when he blows bubbles in the suds.

When we're in the bath together

we're just the best of buds.

Made in the USA
Middletown, DE
19 December 2016